# A LEAP OF FAITH
## ~ *A Novelette*~

# Tam Yvonne

Published By: Pen Legacy®
Layout & Formatting By: Junnita Jackson
Edited By: Carla Dean, U Can Mark My Word Editorial Services
Cover Design & Layout: Junnita Jackson


Library of Congress Cataloging – in- Publication Data has been applied for.

ISBN: 978-1-7351424-8-7

# Preface

My dear readers, I want to first thank you for selecting this book to add to your collection of Christian fiction. Getting this literary piece from my laptop to your hands has been a long journey—a journey that started back in late 2010. I finished writing *A Leap of Faith* in the Spring of 2011. However, by the time the book was done, so was my marriage. Because of my marriage's decline, I put the book on hold and started focusing on what my next move in life would be. At that time, I was residing on the outskirts of Charlotte, North Carolina, with my now ex-husband and two children who were under the age of five. It took me approximately a year to get out of my marriage and relocate myself and two small children back to the Metro Atlanta area near family and friends. It took me another five years to accept my new norm and get things on track for my children and me.

During my time of transition, I watched as my friend, IOTA sorority sister, and now my publisher, Charron Monaye, flourished with her writing career, and I wanted the same for myself. I would often reach out to my sister/soror and ask her questions regarding publishing a book. Even during my most difficult times, my desire to publish *A Leap of Faith* was always on my mind. Charron never pushed me away and always made it her

business to respond to my inquiries. In my mind, I knew I wasn't financially in a place to publish a book. After all, I was raising two children on one income. Still, I kept dreaming, and by contacting Charron, it kept my hope alive.

Because of my strong faith, I knew what I was going through would pass, and eventually, I would be in a position to have everything meant for me. Just as I believed they would, things started coming together for me. During this time, I tried my hand at dating but have no success stories to share with you. I had a few not-so-great jobs but ended up landing with an agency I enjoyed reporting to for work. I started back being active in my church home. My children continued to excel in school, and I purchased our first home in 2018.

After purchasing our home, I started thinking about *A Leap of Faith* again and how it was my goal to get it published in 2019. Well, readers, 2019 came and went, and still no book. My job, my kids, and my church consumed my life so much that I put this book on the back burner for a second time. It took COVID-19, the pandemic of 2020, and my working from home to pick up my manuscript again. I fell in love with this story all over again, and I knew 2020 had to be the year that I published this book. My promise to myself was that if the Lord saw fit for my loved ones and me to make it through the pandemic, I would no longer allow my gift of storytelling to go to waste. I vowed to do everything in my power to get my book published, and finally, the day came when I reached out to Charron Monaye again to inquire about how I could get my book published by the end of 2020. As always, she was there for me and excited to instruct me on what I needed to do to make this happen. After telling her that I had finished my manuscript nine years prior, she was stunned I had been sitting on it for this long, and for me, the process of publishing got easier because the hard work of writing the manuscript was done. At the recommendation of my publisher, she and I agreed on a release date of November 19th, which will be the day of my 45th birthday.

Although I have yet to find my one true love, I have always been a hopeless romantic. You will see that once you start to read my story. I wrote *A Leap of Faith* for all the women who have lost faith in finding true love at one point in their life. I find comfort in knowing that God did not mean for us to spend this precious life alone; He made that plain to us in Genesis 2:18. It just takes some of us longer to be found than others. Please do not lose the faith, though. True love will find you at the right time, and it'll be more than you ever imagined. So, when it comes (and it will come), be ready to take that leap!

In the meantime, I hope my book can be a blessing to you during your time of being still and letting GOD write your love story.

# Acknowledgements

This book could not have been written without the love, patience, and support of my two children, Sharon and Ellis, who are the best children any parent could be blessed to have.

I would also like to take this opportunity to acknowledge my family, especially my sister, La Toya, who has always been that listening ear for me and my voice of reason. She truly helped me through some difficult times in my life, and I could never repay her for her love and kindness towards not only me but also my children. GOD did a good thing when he made us sisters! My handsome nephews, PJ, Bryson, Kevin, and Kyler; my beautiful mother, Christine, for all her sacrifices and teachings; my handsome brothers, Larry Sebastian and Decobie; and my stepfather, Thomas.

I would also like to give a special shout out to a man who has been consistent in my life and who has shown me a positive example of what a good man of God/Jehovah is supposed to be. He is a husband, a father, a friend, a relative, and an all-around standup guy. That person is my uncle Sam. His consistent love, support, and encouragement for me have never wavered, and for that, I am forever grateful.

Thank you to my other uncles, Toney and Gerald; my aunt Mary Ann; my best friend and godmother to my children, Kimberly; my brother-in-love, Glenn; sister-in-love, Jillian; my bishop/pastor of over fourteen years, Bishop Frances V. Mills, and my Tabernacle of Faith Christian Church family; and my loyal friends and family members who have always been TEAM TAM!

Before closing out my acknowledgments, I cannot forget my late grandmother, Mrs. Willie Alma Tate-Curtis, who unselfishly and unconditionally loved and supported me until the day the Lord called her home. Her spirit will live on within me for the rest of my days here on Earth. My late grandfather, Mr. Samuel Curtis, Sr.; the late author, Mrs. Bebe Moore Campbell, who I met in the mid-90s at Augusta College for a book signing (Brothers & Sisters). Her warm smile and kind words always stuck with me. When I expressed to her that I wanted to write just like her, she smiled and said, "You can do it."

Finally, the phenomenal Charron Monaye and Pen Legacy Publishing team, thank you all for taking a chance on an unknown writer, who only wrote for leisure and never thought her book would get out to share with the world. You made a lifelong dream a reality!

# Dedication

This book is dedicated to my Lord and Savior, Jesus Christ, without whom NONE of this would be possible. And to you, the  readers of this book, may you be inspired by my efforts.

"I don't like fond. It sounds like something you would tell a dog. Give me LOVE, or nothing."

~Alice Walker~

# Young, Gifted & Black

It was another Monday morning at Spelman College, and Leilani Michele Bassett was sitting on the steps in front of Packard Hall. The weather was chilly, and she felt like crap. After all, Leilani had stayed up past midnight studying for her chemistry exam. But, being a loyal friend, she agreed to go to breakfast off-campus with her best friend, Allison, who lived in an apartment near campus.

She was waiting for her friend's white 1995 BMW 325i two-door convertible to pull up in front of her dorm's building to pick her up so they could go to the local soul food restaurant for breakfast.

The Q was the hot spot for local college students. The restaurant had the best homemade biscuits around, and the salmon croquettes and grits made you want to "slap your mama," as some of the students would tease. The food reminded you of your grandmother in the kitchen throwing down, and eating there always made Leilani happy because it made her reminisce about her grandmother's cooking when she was a child growing up in a small Georgia town. Students and locals would frequently form lines outside the door to the restaurant, waiting to get in to eat.

As the sun began to shine a little brighter, and the chill of the morning air started to warm, Leilani closed her eyes and leaned forward, resting her head on her knees. She started thinking about her childhood in the small Georgia town with a population of only 2,500 people. She was the daughter of a popular, local African Methodist Episcopal (AME) pastor and an elementary school principal.

Leilani was the only child of Bishop Ervin Bassett and Dr. Almah Mae Connor-Bassett. Her parents were college sweethearts. Her father had attended Morehouse College in Atlanta, Georgia, and her mother right next door at Spelman College. Hence, it was already written that she would be a Spelman woman and marry a Morehouse man.

Leilani grew up very sheltered and lived in a very affluent African American neighborhood. All her friends came from high society families, with parents who were well educated, from doctors to lawyers, pastors to retired military officers, and educators.

For years, her parents tried to have a baby, but with no success, until Leilani's mother's 40th birthday. Dr. Connor-Bassett thought she was battling the flu because of nausea, headaches, and the slight cough she had been

4

experiencing over a few months. Eventually, the headaches and cough went away, but she couldn't shake the nausea. So, at the insistence of her husband, she scheduled a doctor's appointment.

When the appointment arrived, she thought her doctor would tell her that she was overworking and just needed some rest. At that time, Leilani's mother taught 5th-grade arithmetic, and her father was teaching theology at a historically black college in the city's neighboring town. Little did they know she was pregnant with a baby girl.

Leilani was the joy of her parents' eyes, learning to read by age three, playing piano at age four, and speaking words in a foreign language by the time she started kindergarten in the mid-80s at age five.

There was nothing her parents would not do to make sure she had the best of everything. By the time Leilani reached high school, she was known in her community as the top student in her area. She was Valedictorian of her graduating class, a classical pianist, high school cheerleader, a National Honors scholar, a Future Business Leader of America, and a debutante.

By the time she graduated high school in the 90s, she had the likes of Howard University, Hampton University, New York University, Stanford University, Emory University, and many other colleges and universities throwing scholarships to attend
their institutions of higher learning. Although very flattering, Leilani knew Spelman was the college for her, and she gladly accepted their academic scholarship to attend the private, liberal arts, women's college in Atlanta, Georgia.

5

Allison finally arrived, startling Leilani who was almost dozing on the steps of her dorm.

"Girl, you're looking a mess. I mean, no lip gloss or anything, Lani?"

"Gee, thanks, Allie," Leilani said with a sigh as she got in Allison's BMW.

"You okay? I'm serious, you look all tired and stuff."

"I'm good, Allie. I was just up studying all night. I have my chemistry mid-term this afternoon, and you know chemistry is not my thing."

"Okay, then. I don't worry myself over my academics like that. Heck, if I get it, I get it. If not, Daddy will just have to pay for me to retake it. Point. Blank. Period," replied the skinny, light-brown girl, with green eyes and long honey-blonde hair.

Allison Gallant referred to herself as a black, wealthy, and privileged diva. The youngest of two children, she grew up on the east side of the San Francisco Bay in Berkeley, California. Her brother was five years older than she and a law student at Harvard Law School in Cambridge, Massachusetts.

Her father was a superior court judge in Alameda County, California, and her mother died having her during childbirth. Allison made it her business to let anyone who came into her presence know that she was rich and beautiful. Some would call her bourgeois because of her materialistic attitude.

However, deep down, she was a sweet girl who was just looking for people to like her. Leilani immediately saw past all her pretentiousness when they met freshman year in English 101 class.

A strong breezed blew through Allison's car window, and Leilani smiled as a New Edition song came on the radio. Allison turned the volume up loudly, and they both began singing along to "If It Isn't Love."

"This is my song!" Allison yelled over the music.

With the windows down and their hair blowing all over, the girls sang at the top of their lungs with not a care in the world. Life was indeed grand when you were young, gifted, and black.

# Spelman Sisters Forever

"Girl, I cannot believe college is over." Allison sighed while helping Leilani seal her last box before her parents arrived.

The movers that Leilani's parents hired had already loaded her other belongings into the truck. "I know, Allie. It feels like just yesterday we were these little eighteen-year-olds. You from Cali, me from Georgia, sitting in freshman orientation listening to the dean tell us to look at the young lady to our right and our left because everyone was not going to make it out the gates of Spelman College with their college degree."

Allison leaned on the box. "I know, and the sad part is a lot of girls didn't."

"I know," Leilani responded. "Spelman is not an easy college. They challenge you here, and a lot of girls just couldn't stick it out. But, thank God, we did. We did it, Allie!"

"Yes, we did, girl!" Allison exclaimed. "But now, we

are on our own, and we won't see each other every day. You are headed to Charlotte, North Carolina, to work with that awesome non-profit organization for homeless women."

"Allie, you won't be far, girl. You're going to North Carolina, too, and will only be two hours from me, working on your graduate degree at Duke University," Leilani replied, walking over to give her pouting friend a big hug.

"I guess you're right, Lani. We could get together every weekend."

"Of course, we can."

Just then, there was a knock at Leilani's dorm door.

"Come in," she replied.

A tall, slim, dark-skinned, distinguished older man entered the room.

"Daddy!" Leilani exclaimed.

"How is my baby girl?" The older man smiled broadly.

"I'm wonderful, Daddy." Leilani beamed while hugging her father.

"And, Miss Gallant, it is always a pleasure to see your beautiful face," the man continued.

"Hi, Bishop Bassett." Allison smiled, hugging Leilani's father.

"Where's Mom?" Leilani asked as she looked at the door, waiting for her mother to enter the room.

"Lani, you know your mother. When she comes to this campus, she must make her rounds to speak with everyone she knows. I left her talking with some friends in the dean's office, but she said she would meet us at the car. All is settled with the movers. I'll take this last box out to the car myself and shall see you in a few," Pastor Bassett responded, then picked up the box and left the two young ladies to say their goodbyes.

"Well, I guess this is it," Allison said.

"Until we meet in North Carolina," Leilani responded.

"No, silly. I mean, this is it for us as college students. No more late-night talks in your dorm room; no more hanging out with our friends; no more late-night Church's chicken runs, and no more early morning breakfast dates at The Q." Allison laughed before adding, "Oh, and we can't forget, no more sneaking over to Morehouse and trying to sneak back into Packard Hall."

Leilani leaned against the wall and smiled. "Aww, the memories."

She truly had the best four years of her life on that college campus—memories and friendships that she knew would stick with her for a lifetime.

"I love you, Lani."

"I love you, Allie. Spelman sisters forever."

"Spelman sisters forever," Allison repeated with a smile.

# Life After College

It was a Wednesday night and a little after seven o'clock in the evening. The bible study taking place in the worship center of Leilani's newfound ministry drew attention from a lot of the young people in the community. They viewed it as a positive place to worship the Lord, and every week, more and more twenty-somethings entered the front doors.

Leilani stood at the front of the room, waiting to begin bible study. She could not believe her eyes at how full the room was getting with people waiting to hear her teach. Leilani loved talking about the Lord. At an early age, she learned how to deliver the word of God by watching her father, the bishop.

In college, she was part of several Christian organizations on and off-campus and the college's gospel glee club. She could not believe that she, a twenty-something woman of God, was drawing this much interest by teaching on something so dear to her—the word of God.

"Good evening, everyone," Leilani began. "It's almost seven-thirty, and I do not want to keep you all in here late tonight. So, let's get started.

"This Wednesday evening, we will cover *God's Amazing Grace*.

But, before we dive right into the lesson, I see some new faces in the building tonight. Please introduce yourselves."

To the left of where Leilani stood, a beautiful young lady with a huge Afro rose from her seat.

"Hi, everyone. My name is Sharice." She smiled, showing off two deep dimples. "I attend college at Johnson C. Smith University, and I was invited to this bible study by my friend, Jaden, who I work with."

"Well, welcome, Sharice. We are so pleased you could join us this evening, and thank you, Jaden, for inviting Sharice to come and fellowship with us." Leilani smiled. "I do hope this will not be your last time joining us."

She looked around the room again and saw another face she did not recognize.

"Do we have any more visitors?" she asked.

Leilani saw the hand of the unfamiliar face rise in the back of the room. Attached to that hand was one of the most handsome men she had ever seen in her entire life.

"Good evening. I am James Jordan," the tall man greeted with a grin.

His black beard and low tapered haircut complemented his smooth dark-chocolate skin, and he was quite fashionable in his jeans, cream-colored blazer, and light pastel-colored shirt.

"I am a writer and news reporter for the *Charlotte Times*, and I'm here to see what all the hype is about surrounding this new ministry and bible study. Word on the street is that you, Miss Bassett, are the next best thing."

Gawking like a child who just saw her celebrity crush, Leilani could not utter a word. She just nodded and smiled. The handsome man continued. "If possible, I would like to interview you after your bible study."

By this time, everyone was looking Leilani, who had not taken her eyes off the beautiful specimen standing at the back of the room.

She pulled herself together, looked around the room at all the eyes on her and responded, "It would be my pleasure, Mr. Jordan. Thank you for joining us tonight."

The man smiled as he took his seat, and Leilani began her Wednesday night bible study lesson.

"Before I close this bible study, I want to leave you all with this," Leilani said while walking around the room. "We should each make Jesus Christ our daily companion. By beholding Him, we become changed. By maintaining a connection with our Lord and Savior Jesus Christ, we will be able to see the light, feel the peace, and experience serenity. God's grace is truly amazing."

Leilani walked back to the front of the room. "So, for next week, I want you all to read Jeremiah 31:3. I will be discussing how to draw closer to God. It's going to be an awesome study. You won't want to miss it," she told them, then said a prayer and closed out bible study.

Afterward, several people came up to her to give praise on how informative her lesson was and how it was a blessing to have someone who could teach the Word in a way that was understandable for all to follow.

Leilani smiled and thought of how blessed she was to have two parents who were educators. Everything she learned, she got from watching them.

After the last person left, James walked from the back of the room where he had been sitting to stand before Leilani, who was placing her materials in her favorite black backpack.

Smiling, he said, "Now I see."

"See what, Mr. Jordan?" Leilani asked, smiling up at him.

"I see what all the hype is about, Miss Bassett. You are amazing. The way you deliver your message and how you capture the attention of these young people is truly short of amazing," he replied, gazing down at the five-foot-two, beautiful, dark brown woman.

"That is very kind of you to say. I just speak from the heart. I love talking about the Lord, and when I love a topic, I can speak on it passionately and knowledgeably without tripping over my words." Feeling bashful, Leilani looked down at her backpack and asked, "So, has the interview already begun?"

"Uh…no. I'm sorry. Would you be willing to go next door to the coffee shop with me for a cup of joe?" James asked.

"Sure." Leilani smiled and threw her backpack on her shoulder.

"Great," James replied with a smile, then opened the door and allowed Leilani to walk in front of him.

"So, what you are saying is that you answered God's calling on your life at an early age?" James asked, taking a sip of his coffee while jotting notes on a notepad.

"Yes," Leilani replied, sitting in front of the handsome man. "I was nine years old. Even at that early age, I knew I wanted to follow the path the Lord laid out for me. I was always impressed with the Word, and having a father who was a pastor, I heard about the Lord every single day of my life and was taught how wonderful HE is. I see how wonderful HE is by all the super things He has done in my life and my parents' life."

She went on to explain how her parents thought they would never have a child. However, at age forty, her mother found out she was pregnant, even after being diagnosed with endometriosis—a disorder where the tissues lining the uterus grow outside of the uterus and on the ovaries, fallopian tubes, and in her mother's case, on her intestines. Despite her mother's health challenges, God stepped in and made their dreams of becoming parents a reality, and they were blessed with a miracle baby.

"So, you went to Spelman?"

"Yes, I did. It was four of the best years of my life,"

"A Spelman woman," James commented, smiling.

"Yes, indeed." Leilani smiled back. "Where did you go to college?"

"H-U! You know!" James chanted.

The two laughed.

"Okay." Leilani nodded. "Howard University. A Bison, I see."

"All day, every day." James smiled bigger, showing his perfectly straight white teeth.

"So, you grew up a PK?" James continued.

Leilani chuckled. "Yes, I'm a preacher's kid."

"And your mother was a principal at an elementary school in Georgia?"

"Yes," Leilani replied. "How about you? Where did you grow up?"

"I certainly did not grow up like you," James began. "I grew up in a single-parent home in Prince Georges County, Maryland. I am the oldest of five boys. My mother was a nurse, and she died when I was fifteen years old. Three of us ended up with our grandparents in Washington, DC, and my youngesttwo brothers went to live with my mother's sister and husband in Richmond, Virginia."

"Wow," Leilani responded. "I'm sure being separated from your younger brothers was hard."

17

"It was," James replied, looking down at his coffee. "Losing my mother was tough, too," he continued. "Cancer is a beast."

"Yes, it is," Leilani agreed.

Seeing the sadness on his face, she wanted to lighten the mood. "So, were you a journalism major in school?"

James laughed. "Heck, no. I was on a football scholarship, and all I wanted to do was play ball and chase girls."

Leilani laughed with him. "What was your major?"

"Honestly, it was undecided for a long time."

Once again, the two began to laugh uncontrollably.

"No, but seriously, I got myself together during my junior year and declared a major of English."

"Nice," Leilani replied, smiling.

"But enough about me, Miss Bassett. Off the record, why is such an attractive woman like yourself not off the market?" James flirted.

"Who said I wasn't off the market, Mr. Jordan?" Leilani responded, flirting back.

"Oh, okay. Excuuuuse me." James laughed. "I mean, I didn't see a ring on your finger."

Leilani smiled at the confident, smart man sitting before her. He was right; she didn't have a ring on her finger. Until that moment, she never really gave it any thought. She consumed herself with working with the homeless women at her non-profit job. When not there, she was doing ministry work. So, she found no time to accept the many offers for dates that she received from some gentleman suitors.

Interrupting her thoughts, James asked, "Did I say something wrong?"

"No, no," Leilani assured him. "I guess I just never thought about my personal life until you brought it up. I haven't had the time to date."

James smiled. "Well, I would like to change that."

Leilani gazed at him. "Really?"

"Yes, really." James smirked.

"May I take you out tomorrow night? Say around seven o'clock?"

"I work until five. Can we do eight instead?"

"Whatever you want, my lady." James smiled. "I just want some of your time."

Leilani's insides were doing flips. She could not believe what was happening. How in the world did someone who seemed to be so special just fall into her lap? It had to be God's doing. She could feel it. She could not wait to call Allison.

"Okay, eight o'clock it is. Do you want me to meet you someplace?" she asked.

"Absolutely not. If you're comfortable with it, I would like to pick you up from your home and take you on a date, Miss Bassett," James replied.

"I'm fine with that," Leilani responded, and then while smiling, she grabbed his notepad and jotted down her address and telephone number.

Just then, a young, thin white guy approached their table in the corner of the coffee shop.

"Excuse me. We will be closing in ten minutes."

19

"Thanks, my man. We are wrapping it up here," James told him.

The young man nodded and walked off.

"Well, let me walk you back to your car and make sure you get there safely," James said, standing up. "I certainly do not want anything happening to the beautiful chocolate princess." He bowed as if he was saluting a queen.

Leilani laughed. "You are something else."

"I am," James agreed, "and you are going to grow to love it."

Once they reached Leilani's car, James opened the driver's side door for her.

"Thank you for your time, Miss Leilani Bassett," he expressed with a grin.

"It was my pleasure," Leilani replied, returning a smile.

It was an awkward silence as they stood there gazing at one another.

Breaking the silence, James replied, "Well, I will see you tomorrow, pretty lady."

"Until tomorrow," Leilani said, then smiled as she got into her car.

"Oh, and I like this Benz." James winked, holding her door open.

"Thanks. It was a graduation gift from my parents," Leilani shyly replied while putting on her seatbelt in her Mercedes Benz C-Class Sedan.

"I'm not mad at you," James teased, closing the door. "Get home safely."

"You, too." Leilani gave him one final smile before driving off into the night.

# First Date

The following workday dragged along slowly. All Leilani could think about was James. His smile. Those perfectly-aligned white teeth. His broad shoulders and beautiful, jet black skin that looked like satin. The black curly hair that was tapered low and laid down on his head. Not to mention how good he smelled as if he walked right out of a Jean Paul Gaultier cologne ad.

Finally, five o'clock rolled around, and Leilani, who was usually the last to leave the office, was the first out the door that afternoon. After all, she had to get ready for her date.

Once at home, she rummaged through her closet. Since James did not tell her where they were going, she could not decide on what would be appropriate to wear. She did not even think to get his telephone number, so calling to ask him was not an option.

"Darn," she thought. "How could I not think to get his number?"

But she knew exactly why. Leilani had not been

thinking clearly that night because she was so taken aback by James' charisma and good looks. From the moment when he stood up at the back of the room during bible study, she lost all control of her senses. Never had she seen a man so intriguing.

She finally decided on a cute, fitted, long-sleeve black dress. Not too provocative, very classy, tasteful, and ladylike. Like her mother would say, "Always be a lady."

When the doorbell rang, Leilani grabbed her blinged black clutch purse that her best friend, Allison, gave her as a birthday gift the year before and ran to get the front door. As she opened the door, James stood before her with a huge grin, holding a bouquet of beautiful red roses.

Leilani smiled, all the while thinking, *What is love at first sight?* At that moment, she felt it existed.

"Wow! You look stunning," James replied.

Bashfully, Leilani said, "Thank you. You clean up very well yourself."

"I try," James responded and laughed.

"So, where are we going? I had no clue what to wear. So, I hope I am not overdressed," Leilani rambled, which she did whenever she was nervous.

James starred down at her petite frame. "You are absolutely perfect. You do not need to change a single thing."

Leilani smiled, took the flowers he offered to her, placed them on the counter, and off they went.

"Dinner was amazing." Leilani expressed as she and James walked through the park, admiring the Charlotte skyline.

"Ruth Chris is one of my favorite restaurants. You can never go wrong with a good steak and lobster tail," James told her, then grabbed hold of Leilani's hand. "Since dinner was so amazing, I think we deserve another amazing date," he added, flashing a smile.

As they strolled along hand-in-hand, Leilani smiled and replied, "Well, that's up to you."

"I'm in," James immediately responded.

"You in?" she asked.

"Yeah."

"Okay," Leilani said, then smiled once more.

"We can do anything. It's up to you," James continued.

"Do you do yoga?" she asked.

"Yooooga?" James dragged out the word with a silly look on his face.

The two stopped and faced each other.

"Yes, YO-GA!" Leilani smiled, moving her hands in the air like a cheerleader chanting a cheer.

"You mean like stretching, twisting, and all of that? On the ground?" James asked.

Leilani laughed. "Uh, yes, that's yoga."

"Umm, okay, yeah," James agreed. "Girl, I'm down with the yoga. Heck, I'm the king of yoga," he replied, holding his arm up and flexing a muscle.

Leilani smiled. "Okay, how about Saturday morning? Nine o'clock, here at the park."

"Cool, I will be here," James replied, grabbing hold of her hand again. "C'mon, woman, let's go."

They walked back to the car.

James walked Leilani to her front door.

"Tonight was great. Thank you," James told her, smiling as he looked down at the beautiful woman.

"Thank you for what?" Leilani asked.

"For accepting my date invitation and for making tonight such an amazing night. You are a phenomenal woman, Leilani, and I want to see more of you," he continued.

Leilani could not believe what she was hearing from this man—the man of her dreams. Everything she wanted in a man was standing right before her.

"Well, thank you for wanting to get to know me, James," Leilani responded as she smiled back at him.

The two stared at each other with an awkward silence between them until James reached down to hug her.

"Until Saturday."

"Until Saturday," she said, then watched him walk down the driveway to his black Lexus LX 570.

The next morning at work, Leilani could not wait to call Allison.

"Girl, where have you been? I have not heard from you in weeks," Allison began. "Are you working that hard?"

"Allie, I have been so busy with my ministry, working with the homeless ladies, and dating the most wonderful guy on the planet," Leilani said, beaming.

"Hold up! DATING? Did I hear you correctly?" Allison shouted through the phone. "I know the little prophetess has not been out on the dating scene."

"Girl, I am not on a dating scene. It is just one guy. This man came to my bible study, and he's a reporter with our local paper. So, he wanted to do a story on me about how my ministry was drawing a lot of attention from the young people, specifically the college students in our area," Leilani explained.

"Uh-huh...and how did the dating come about?" Allison asked, ignoring everything her friend had said.

Leilani laughed. "You are not interested in anything I just said except for the part about dating."

Allison started laughing on the other end of the phone.

"You're right."

"Well, we went for coffee afterward so that James could interview me, but we didn't get a lot of interviewing done because we started talking about our lives, our parents, how we were raised, college. You know, all the basic things. By the time the evening was over, he was asking me on a date, girl." Leilani giggled.

"Okay, then. Well, tell me about him. Is he cute?"

"His name is James Jordan. He's twenty-six years old and from Prince Georges County, Maryland. He is a Howard University graduate, and cute is an understatement. This man is GORGEOUS, girl!" Leilani exclaimed. "He has the smoothest chocolate skin I have ever seen in my life. His teeth are perfectly straight and pearly white, like ivory, and his hair is just as black as his skin. Girl, it's like he stepped off the country of Mother Africa. And get this, Allie."

"What girl?" Allison asked excitedly.

"He's tall, and I'm not talking this, 'Oh I'm six foot tall.'"

"How tall, girl?" Allison interrupted.

"Six-five," Leilani squealed.

Both ladies started screeching on the phone like two teenagers who just found out the other had gotten her first kiss from a boy.

"Oh my! That is tall," Allison responded.

"But it's not just his looks, Allie. He is such a gentleman. He is smart, funny, and so sweet," Leilani explained. "And he has a real job. Allie, this one is a keeper."

"Hold on. Wait a minute, Lani. How long have you known this guy? Wasn't this the first date?" Allison asked with uneasiness. "I mean, I'm sure he is a good guy and everything, but you just met him. You already sound like you're in love, girl."

"Allison, I didn't say anything about love," Leilani replied, rubbing the top of the coffee mug she was holding. "But he is the kind of man I can see myself with."

Allison was quiet on the other end of the phone.

"Look, Allie, I can't remember the last time I have been this hopeful about a guy," Leilani continued.

"Okay, Lani. Just take your time. I don't want you to get hurt. I'm sure, James—that is his name, right?"

"Yes."

"Well, I'm sure James is a great guy, and I can't wait to meet him the next time I'm in Charlotte."

"Thanks, girl," Leilani answered.

"Well, I have to get off this phone. Some of us have work to do," Allison joked. "I love you, sis."

"Love you, too. We'll talk soon."

Both ladies hung up the phone.

"Good morning, beautiful," James greeted.

Leilani had left work to meet him in the parking lot of the park.

She smiled and replied, "Good morning. Are you ready?"

"Of course. Remember, I'm the king of yoga," James bragged, flexing his muscles.

Leilani laughed, and the two found a secluded area of the park where they could lay down their yoga mats. She had brought a mini radio to play calming music and two bottles of water. As the two stretched and prepared to do their yoga workout, Leilani began to giggle.

"What's so funny, Miss Bassett?" James asked, looking over at her with her head on her upper thighs as she effortlessly touched her toes.

"You, Mr. King of Yoga." She laughed, flexing her muscles as he had done. "It looks like you're struggling to touch your toes."

"Nah, I'm good," he responded, barely reaching his ankles.

"Are you sure? It doesn't look like it." She laughed harder. "You know we could walk the park instead."

James laughed and got up, then reached to grab her hands and pull her up. "That would be a heck of a lot better than me trying to touch my toes."

The two laughed and started walking the park.

"It's such a beautiful day," Leilani said, enjoying the cool breeze and lovely sounds of the birds chirping.

"Not as beautiful as you," James commented with a smile.

The two stopped and looked at each other.

"I truly hope I'm not the only one who had an amazing time the other night," James continued.

Leilani nodded. "It was amazing."

She inched in closer to him, and James pulled her to him, bent down, and kissed her. It had been a long time since Leilani had not felt that type of urge in her body. She slowly pulled away from his gentle grip.

30

They proceeded to walk again until they were back where they started. Leilani walked over to their mats and sat down, James next to her.

"You want a bottle of water?" she asked, handing him one of the two she had brought.

"Of course," he replied, taking the bottle from her hand.

The two took a sip of their water in silence.

"Cold," he said, smiling. "I needed this."

She nodded. "I'm glad you like."

"Look, Leilani, I haven't stopped thinking about you since our first exchange at your church."

"Trust me, I know the feeling," she responded while looking into his mesmerizing brown eyes.

"Good. At least I don't look like a fool," he continued.

Speechless, the two just stared at one another until Leilani directed her gaze down at her water bottle.

"James, I think there's something wonderful happening here."

"I agree," he responded, looking at her.

The two chatted for about an hour or so about life, hopes, and dreams.

"Is it already noon?" Leilani asked.

"Yes, it is, and I have a one-thirty meeting at the office," James replied, standing up and grabbing both mats.

After Leilani stood up, James bent over and placed another kiss on her lips. Leilani pressed her body into his, with strong hands holding her waist.

This time, he pulled away first. "You're going to get me in trouble," he joked, then placed a gentle kiss on her forehead.

Leilani smiled.

He walked her back to her car and placed the yoga workout equipment in the trunk.

Holding open her car door, he replied, "Have a good day, Miss Bassett."

"You, too, Mr. Jordan." Leilani smiled. *Could this be love?* she thought while driving away.

# The Real Deal

Leilani did not need confirmation from anyone to finally know she had found her husband. An angel came to her in a dream shortly after she and James met the night of her bible study. She had heard the angel clearly say, *You are entertaining your husband. He needs you.* That was all the confirmation Leilani needed.

The more time she spent with James, the more their relationship bloomed. He reminded her of her father with his charm, moral values, and good looks. James was so considerate and courteous, and he always thought about her.

James and Leilani spent a lot of time together, whether they were at her home or his playing Uno or out and about in the city of Charlotte doing something special. They were always together, doing anything to see each other.

Their courtship was short and blossomed rather quickly. There was no doubt they were smitten with one another.

They shared a lot of moments attending church together, taking road trips, meeting each other's families, going to the movies, concerts, ballets, and plays. They did everything together.

Leilani had fallen in love with James' heart more than his handsome good looks.

"Hi, sweetie," Leilani answered, holding her cell phone.

"Hi, beautiful. Are you free tonight? I want to make you dinner," James replied on the other end of the phone.

"I am. What are we having?" Leilani asked.

"We're having my famous Jamaican jerk chicken, rice and peas, plantains, and cabbage," James responded in a fake Jamaican accent.

"Wow! What's the occasion?" Leilani inquired, impressed with the dinner menu.

James was a great cook and attributed his cooking skills to his late mother, who loved cooking for him and his brothers. He said he would often sit on a stool in their kitchen and watch her cook. That was their bonding time together.

"You," James responded. "You are the special occasion."

Leilani smiled. "I'll be there at six."

"Oh my gosh, baby. Dinner was scrumptious. I knew you could cook, but you outdid yourself tonight." Leilani smiled while giving James a big hug from behind as he stood at his kitchen sink washing the dishes.

"Thank you, my love. Anything for you," he replied, turning to face her. "Wait right here for a sec."

James left the kitchen for a moment and returned shortly, handing Leilani a little blue-green box. As she accepted the box, he dropped to his knee.

Leilani's heart began to beat fast; she could barely hear herself think. *Oh my gosh, is this really happening?* she thought.

"Leilani Michele Bassett, will you do me the honor of being my wife?" James asked, looking up at the petite, beautiful woman standing in front of him with tears in her eyes.

Leilani opened the Tiffany jewelry box and pulled out a stunning ring. It was simple, just like she liked, and very gorgeous. Taking the ring from her, he slipped it on her finger. It fit perfectly.

With tears streaming down her face, she answered, "Of course, I'll marry you!"

That next morning, Leilani called her parents and Allison to share her good news. Everyone was so excited for her and James.

# Jumping the Broom

"Girl, we have a wedding to plan," Allison replied, sitting at Leilani's dining room table, pulling up wedding websites on her laptop.

Leilani was so excited. Like most little girls, Leilani often daydreamed about getting married to her Prince Charming and living happily ever after like Cinderella. By the time she was twelve years old, she had everything planned out, but now that the time was here, she was clueless about where to begin. It was as if it was her first time thinking about a wedding. So, she was grateful to have her best friend, her Spelman sister, there to help her.

James and Leilani had agreed to have a small, intimate, spring wedding in the Blue Ridge Mountains of North Carolina. That way, things at work would be slow for both of them, and all their family members would be able to attend.

In the days following their engagement, James and Leilani discussed wedding ideas and planning their life together. The two shared their dreams and hopes about their marriage, their love for each other, and starting a family. They both wanted two children—a girl for her and a boy for him.

Wanting their union to have a strong foundation, they took premarital counseling at their church to discuss some typical issues that pertained to marriage.

At last, spring arrived, and so did the wedding of James Barry Jordan and Leilani Michele Bassett.

On the morning of her wedding, Leilani woke up feeling excited. She was calm, no jitters, but ready to marry the man of her dreams. She knew it was all right in God's eyes and that she was marrying the man who HE had assigned to her.

They had invited over one hundred people to the wedding scheduled to start at two-thirty in the afternoon. Neither Leilani nor James had over-the-top personalities; therefore, the ceremony would be simple but elegant.

James had gotten up extra early that morning to get a haircut with Stuart, who was his best man and best friend. The two had played football together in college, and they were also Omega fraternity brothers.

James wore a white top underneath a light gray suit perfectly tailored to fit his tall, athletic frame. His friend,

Stuart, who looked like the young version of the Motown singer, Marvin Gaye, stood next to him dressed in a similar suit.

On the front row alongside Leilani's mother sat James' aunt, Gloria, and his uncle Roscoe, Gloria's husband who raised James' younger brothers when their mother passed away. Standing at the front of the chapel near the pastor was Leilani's best friend, Allison, looking as beautiful as ever in a long, soft pink, flowy, mesh high-neck halter bridesmaid gown, with her long hair pulled up in a high bun.

When James looked up, he saw Leilani in her wedding dress for the first time, and he could not believe his eyes. His reaction to her was the most poignant sight ever. She was the most beautiful woman he had ever seen.

She wore an A-line, ivory lace, Bohemian-style, backless wedding dress with a deep V-neck illusion outlined with appliques.

As James watched her walk down the aisle with her father, tears began to well in his eyes. *How did I get so lucky?* he thought.

Once Leilani and her father finally made it to the front of the chapel, the officiant asked, "Who giveth this woman to this man?"

Leilani's father replied, "Her mother and I do." Then Bishop Bassett handed Leilani's hand to James, kissed his daughter on her cheek, and gave James a handshake before taking a seat next to his wife on the front row.

Leilani and James remained calm during their wedding ceremony. However, James did get choked up while reciting his wedding vows to Leilani.

After exchanging vows, James slipped the most stunning wedding band onto Leilani's finger. Next, Leilani slipped on his finger a beautiful black wedding band she had purchased for him. Then the officiant pronounced them husband and wife and stated it was time to salute the bride, and James did just that. He did not care who was present; he kept kissing Leilani until Stuart joked, "Save all that for the honeymoon."

The couple ended their ceremony by jumping over a beautifully crafted broomstick wrapped in pink and gray ribbon to signify their entrance together into a new life.

After the wedding, the guests did not have to go far. The reception hall was right next door and decorated beautifully with Leilani and James' wedding colors. Ever since she was a little girl, Leilani loved flowers. So, her mother and father, who paid for the wedding, made sure there were flowers everywhere. It was simply beautiful!

Leilani and James' first dance together as husband and wife was to Jesse Powell's "You": *Starting here today I surrender all my loveI never thought I could I'm giving all my love away And there's only one reason that I would And baby it's you*

James and Leilani had the most wonderful time dancing to their first song, and the reception turned out to be a huge success. It was a big party with lots of laughter, dancing, eating, and fun for all!

That day was a celebration of them becoming one unto GOD before all of their family and friends. It was a day neither of them would ever forget and one they believed they would cherish forever.

But, as they say, good times don't last always...

# The Doctor Said What?

"What is it, Doctor?" Leilani asked.

She sat nervously with James in a cold, white office at the local hospital, awaiting the physician's response.

"I've thought about how to tell you this, but there is no easy way," began the middle-aged African American woman. Her long, neatly groomed, auburn-colored dreadlocks swayed as she spoke.

Leilani and James had received a call from his physician to come into the office regarding his recent physical examination.

The two had been married four months. Right after they returned from their honeymoon in Negril, Jamaica, James informed Leilani that he was experiencing pain whenever he urinated, and at times, he could not stop the urination.

Although Leilani felt it probably wasn't anything serious, she had urged him to go to the doctor to get it checked out, but James kept putting it off. However, when he started having difficulties getting an erection and saw blood in his semen and urine, he decided not to wait any longer. His doctor ran many tests and had finally gotten the results.

With a solemn expression, the physician continued, "Your results came back, Mr. Jordan. It's cancer. Prostate."

Leilani's eyes widened, and she gasped in disbelief as James sat in silence.

"Mr. Jordan, I had my lab technician run your test three times to make sure the results were accurate, and each time, it came back positive. I'm so sorry."

James finally spoke up. "What does this mean?"

"Because the cancer has spread to your bones, you will need immediate treatment," the doctor continued.

Leilani began to sob. She knew with the cancer reaching his bones that it made her husband's situation even more severe.

James grabbed her hand to comfort her.

"We will need to start chemotherapy as soon as next week," the doctor replied, then handed James several brochures on prostate cancer and scheduled his first chemotherapy appointment.

"Allison, I don't know what to do," Leilani cried. "I can't lose him."

"Sweetie, don't think that way. It may not be as serious as it sounds," Allison said, trying to comfort her friend.

"Allie, we both know once it spreads to your organs and bones, it's pretty much a done deal," Leilani said, weeping harder.

Ever since James' diagnosis with prostate cancer, all she did was cry. She wanted to be strong for her husband, but she just couldn't pull herself together. The thought of losing him always won, and it made her cry every time she thought about what her husband was going through.

She couldn't help but think that he had been ill for a long time and just didn't want to tell her to protect her feelings. James had always thought about her before he thought about himself. A former high school and college football player, James was a strong man and had a Superman mentality—thinking he could beat anything. As her protector, he did not want her to fear anything, and therefore, he thought he would be able to fight what he was battling inside his body.

Feeling helpless on how to comfort her best friend, Allison remained silent on the other end of the telephone line.

Finally, she found the words to say, "Don't cry, honey. You have to be strong for James."

"Come on, baby. You have to eat something."

45

Leilani tried to assist James with eating soup, but he had no appetite. The chemotherapy treatments he had been undergoing for the past month had robbed him of his appetite, among other things. He began losing weight rapidly, and the disease zapped him of all his energy. He didn't even look like the same man she had dated and eventually married. But, the love he had for her still surfaced in his eyes every time she looked at him.

Despite the treatments, the cancer was moving rapidly throughout his body, and the doctors had given him six weeks to live. Leilani had never had her faith tested the way it was being tested with James' illness.

One night, James got up to use the bathroom, and she heard a loud thump. He had fallen in the bathroom and could not get up. She immediately called an ambulance, and they rushed him to the county hospital. That was the beginning of the end.

Leilani worked tirelessly at her jobs with the homeless women and her ministry, but she still managed to find the time to visit James every day in the hospital.

She would read to him, sing to him, and feed him. She did not allow the nurses to bathe him; she wanted to do it herself. Oftentimes, she would lay with him in his hospital bed, and they would watch television together. With his head resting on her shoulder, she cuddled him like a mother would a small child.

One night, while she and James were sitting in his hospital room listening to music on the radio and reminiscing about how they met, their wedding song came on—"You" by Jesse Powell.

Because cancer had taken most of his energy, James did not talk much, but that evening, he managed to whisper for Leilani to come closer and dance with him as he sat up in his hospital bed.

She sat on his bed, put her arms around his neck, and he held her close as they moved slowly to the music.

Leilani began to cry. She could hear her husband struggling to breathe, but he would not let her go.

As the song played, he whispered in her ear, "I will forever be with you, my dear Lani."

"Shush." She tried to quiet him, not wanting him to use too much energy trying to speak.

"My time," he continued, "is drawing near."

Tears began to fall down Leilani's face.

"I don't want you to go, James. I love you. I need you."

"It's time."

"Please, don't say that, James."

"Promise me you will be happy. Don't cry for me. I am in God's hands."

"James, please…" Leilani wept, shaking her head.

"All the love you have, please promise to love again," James replied weakly.

Leilani did not respond. She felt so lost and could not stop crying.

"Lani?"

"Yes, James," she whispered.

"Please love again. I love you and will always be with you."

She kissed his forehead and laid his head down on his pillow as the song on the radio ended.

Leilani sat in the chair beside his bed, holding his hand until she fell asleep. The next morning when she awoke, he was gone.

# He's Gone

"Mom, I cannot believe he's gone," Leilani said, sobbing. "Why? Why did God take my husband?"

"Leilani Michele, you know your father and I did not raise you to question God. I know you are hurting, baby, but you never question the work of the Lord," replied Leilani's mother, who rubbed her daughter's head.

As Leilani laid with her head on her mother's lap, she started thinking about how inseparable she and James had been. Not knowing how she was going to handle him not being there with her, she began to weep.

James' funeral arrangements were simple. Being a simple man, he wanted little fanfare. So, respecting her late husband's wishes, she had a graveside memorial service for him with family and only a few close friends present.

As Leilani's mother continued to stroke her hair, she whispered, "Darling, I think it will do you some good to speak with a grief counselor."

Leilani didn't say anything in response, but she knew her mother was right. She would speak with someone, but at that moment, all she wanted was her mother and just to cry.

# How Do I Move On?

Leilani sat at the table in the restaurant, sticking her fork in and out of her salad but never putting the food to her lips. The past six months had been difficult for her with James gone.

She had buried James in Maryland and started grief counseling with an excellent therapist who was recommended by one of her church members. Leilani made the hard decision to leave her job at the non-profit organization where she had worked to help homeless women for many years. Now she could devote her time to her ministry full-time, which was growing tremendously.

Life was looking good for her, but she could not shake the fact that James was not there to share in her happiness and successes. She had looked forward to sharing life's goodness with her husband, but he was taken too soon.

"Lani, are you okay?" asked Allison.

"I'm fine. Why?" Leilani quickly replied, looking up from her salad.

"You've been picking at your food for the past five minutes. Is there something on your mind?" her concerned friend inquired.

Leilani took in a deep breath. "Allie, I'm trying so hard to move on with my life. My counselor recommended staying busy, so I've been throwing myself into my work. And since Daddy's diagnosis with Alzheimer's, I've spent more time with my parents down in Georgia. I have been doing everything possible to keep my mind off James not being here, but when I am home..." Tears began to well in her eyes. "...home alone, James is all I think about."

"Oh, Lani, it's still fresh in your mind, honey. James was a good man, and he was good to you. It's normal for you to be feeling the way you feel," Allison responded, grabbing Leilani's hand across the table. "We don't know why God does what HE does, but you can believe everything is done for a reason. It will get better for you. Who knows? You might find another man that will make you feel like James made you feel."

Shaking her head, Leilani responded, "No, Allie. I will never love another the way I loved James. I will not allow myself to disrespect his memory or what we had."

"Lani, I'm not saying you will love another the way you loved James, but you can't give up your life and your chance at love again because the Lord called your husband home. Everyone deserves to be loved and to give love. Weren't you the one who told me that James' last words to you were for you to love again?" Allison asked.

Pressing her lips together, Leilani responded, "I know, Allie, but I just can't. I can't see myself with another man."

Hating that her friend was in so much pain, Allison watched as a tear rolled down Leilani's cheek.

"Lani, I'm not saying right now at this moment, but never say never," Allison replied, handing her friend a tissue. "What God has for you is for you, and you will get it. It will be up to you to receive it."

Leilani sighed deeply and took a sip of her diet cola.

"Never, Allie. Never."

"The message for today is reaching forth," Prophetess Leilani began.

She stood in front of her congregation in the packed church.

"Amen," the congregation responded in unison.

"As Philippians 3:13 specifically states, *'Brethren, I count not myself to have apprehended: but this one thing I do, forgetting those things which are behind, and reaching forth unto those things which are before.'*

"Church, we go through things in our lives that we think we will never get over. We encounter people and situations that we think we will NEVER overcome," Leilani energetically spoke. "But I am here today to tell you, children of God, that you can forget those things behind you and reach and look forward to the marvelous things that are before you. All of your worries, God's got it!"

The church erupted in applause.

"Choir, I feel like hearing 'God's Got It'," Leilani shouted, looking behind her to the church choir who exploded in song.

Leilani sat down in her purple chair on the pulpit and closed her eyes as the choir sang the selection she requested. *What a mighty God we serve*, she thought.

"Girl, you outdid yourself with that sermon today," Allison expressed.

Allison had relocated to the Charlotte area after graduating from Duke University's business school with her graduate degree. She knew her best friend would need her. So, she landed a job in Charlotte and accepted it.

"Thanks, Allie. I wasn't as prepared today as I typically am. I just spoke what was on my heart, girl. God is so good. HE let the words flow from my mouth today, and I just followed his lead." Leilani smiled while flipping the television channels and holding her telephone to her ear.

"Well, I know that message today touched a lot of souls, including mine," Allison continued.

"I'm glad it did, and I am glad I was able to do what the Lord wanted me to do," Leilani responded, smiling. "Now, all I need to do is find myself another keyboard player."

"Another keyboard player? What's up with that young man who plays now?" Allison asked. "He's fantastic."

"Lance is great, but he just received a full scholarship to Princeton University. So, he'll be leaving for New Jersey within the next week," Leilani replied. "Don't get me wrong. I'm happy for him. He's such an intelligent young man with a bright future, and you and I both know these colleges are not giving out full scholarships every day. So, it's a great opportunity for him."

"Wow! That's great! I know his parents are thrilled," Allison exclaimed.

"They are. His mother was a little nervous about him going to New Jersey, but after speaking with me, she felt a little more comfortable. I told her that he will be fine. He'll find a good church home and become active again," Leilani said. "Now, I have to place an ad for a keyboardist."

"Don't be too hasty. You might not have to place that ad," Allison began. "I actually know a remarkable keyboardist who is seeking a part-time gig with a church."

"Really? Tell me more," replied Leilani.

"His name is Floyd Hamilton. He and I serve on the same executive board for a non-profit real estate organization I'm affiliated with," Allison continued. "He's a nice guy and very talented. Not to mention, he's single and handsome. Girl, Idris has nothing on Floyd."

"Don't go there, Allie. I need a keyboardist, not a man," Leilani responded with a groan. "Do you think he could meet me tomorrow around 4:30 for an interview?"

"I can call him tonight and get back with you," Allison replied.

"If it's a go, just have him meet me at the church. I'll be there anyway, and Janice, the receptionist, will have instructions where to direct him," Leilani told her. "Tell him to bring two church selections, traditional and non-traditional, that he enjoys playing."

"I certainly will," Allison said, then sniggered.

"Why are you sniggering?" Leilani asked.

"Oh, nothing," Allison mocked. "I just know you two are going to hit it off. Floyd is a cool guy. You'll see."

"C'mon, Allie, don't go there. I'm not looking for love. I just want another good keyboardist to replace Lance, that's all," Leilani explained.

"Yeah, yeah, I hear you, Prophetess Leilani Jordan." Allison laughed aloud. "I'll wait for my 'thank you' when you two hit it off."

Leilani laughed. "Go to bed, girl. I'll talk to you after I interview him."

"*Him* has a name, and his name is Floyd. Get used to saying that, and I'll be waiting for your call. Love you, girl. Goodnight," Allison replied, hanging up the phone.

Leilani laid back on the sofa to finish watching the evening news. However, she could not help but think about her conversation with Allison. *What if Floyd is a good man? What if I find myself attracted to him when I meet him? Should I call Allison back and cancel the interview?*

She had to go into deep prayer on this one.

"Lord, guide my steps," she spoke aloud, "and let Your will be done. Amen."

58

# The Keyboardist

"Prophetess Jordan, a Mr. Floyd Hamilton is waiting for you in your office," replied the jolly, middle-aged receptionist, her salt-and-pepper hair styled in a short bob.

"Thank you, Janice. Did you offer him a beverage?" Leilani asked while retrieving her mail out of the basket on the receptionist's desk.

"Yes, ma'am, but he said he did not want anything," the woman replied.

"Thank you, Janice. You're such a blessing to this ministry," Leilani told her, then smiled and winked at her diligent receptionist.

Leilani couldn't help but think about her conversation with Allison the night before, but she dismissed those thoughts as she entered her office. Once inside, she was greeted by a bald, caramel-colored, attractive man who was medium height and had an athletic build.

*Allie didn't lie,* Leilani thought as she smiled at the handsome man standing before her.

"Mr. Hamilton, I presume?"

"Yes," he replied, smiling back.

"I'm Prophetess Leilani Jordan," she said, introducing herself as she extended her hand.

"Nice to meet you, Prophetess Jordan." The man grabbed hold of her hand and shook it firmly. "Please, call me Floyd," he told her in a smooth, velvety tone.

"Floyd, it is a pleasure to meet you," Leilani began, sliding her hand from his. "Let's chat before I hear your selections."

She walked behind her desk, and he took a seat in front of her.

"Allison Gallant recommended you. Ms. Gallant and I have been friends for years. Well, we're more than friends. We're more like sisters, and she knows what I like. So, for her to recommend you as a great keyboardist, I trust I am going to enjoy your ability to play."

"Yes, Allison and I have been on an executive board or two together for a few years. She is a very no-nonsense woman, and I imagine you are the same way—all about your business," Floyd responded.

Leilani nodded.

"I was honored when she recommended me for this opportunity," Floyd continued. "I have heard marvelous things about your ministry."

Tapping her fingers together, Leilani replied, "You've heard of my ministry, and yet, I cannot recall seeing you here to worship with us."

"Up until recently, I've been working two jobs to finish my graduate degree, and when I did get a Sunday off

60

from my studies, I would attend my mother's church, which is my family's home church. I haven't had a chance to fellowship with many churches in the area," Floyd explained.

"So you're completing your graduate degree? May I ask in what?" Leilani inquired.

"I'm a stockbroker by trade, but I'm completing a Master of Business Administration in Real Estate. I own a few real estate properties in and around the city. You may have heard of Hamilton Homes, Incorporated."

Leilani nodded. "I have seen the billboards and signs around. You're quite the popular one in this area."

"I try." Floyd flashed a beautiful smile that almost blinded her.

"Well, I don't want to continue prying into your business. That's not why you're here. You're here to show your talent," Leilani quickly responded, not wanting to be hypnotized by Floyd's beautiful smile. "What selections have you brought with you this afternoon?"

"Allison informed me that you wanted a traditional and a non-traditional selection," Floyd began. "So, for the traditional selection, I'm going to play 'Take My Hand, Precious Lord' written by the great Reverend Thomas A. Dorsey, and the non-traditional selection is one by BeBe and CeCe Winans called 'Lost Without You'."

"Two of my favorites." Leilani smiled. "The keyboard is set-up for you," she continued, pointing to the corner of the room by the window where the facilities manager had placed a portable keyboard and chair. "Whenever you're ready," she told him.

With his music in hand, Floyd stood to his feet, walked over to the keyboard, and started playing a few notes to warm up.

"Is there a selection you'd like to hear first?" he asked.

"No. Surprise me," Leilani responded, smiling again.

Floyd began playing the notes to "Lost Without You", and he played beautifully.

Leilani closed her eyes to enjoy the music. Then, suddenly, she heard the most beautiful male voice singing the words to the song. She opened her eyes in amazement. Allison told her that he was a good keyboardist, but she didn't say a thing about him being a singer.

Seeing astonishment on her face, Floyd flashed those pearly whites and continued singing while playing the keyboard until the end of the song.

"Wow! You didn't tell me you were a singer, as well," Leilani replied when he finished.

Floyd smiled and responded, "You never asked. I have a lot of talents, and singing is one of them."

A knock on the door interrupted their conversation.

"Prophetess Jordan."

"Janice, do come in," Leilani replied. "Is something wrong?"

"No, ma'am. I'm sorry for interrupting, but I couldn't help but overhear that beautiful song," Janice commented while smiling.

Leilani looked at her receptionist, who appeared fascinated by what she had just heard. "Janice, would you like to sit in and hear Mr. Hamilton's second selection?" Leilani invited.

"Oh, Prophetess Jordan, may I?" Janice asked, taking a seat.

Leilani smiled. "Yes, Janice. Please stay."

As Floyd began playing the notes to "Precious Lord", both ladies were entertained once again by his beautiful voice.

"So will we see you on Sunday?" Leilani asked as she walked Floyd to the front door of the church.

"Yes, you will. I appreciate the opportunity," Floyd responded, extending his hand.

Leilani smiled as she took hold of his smooth hand. "You're very welcome. I appreciate your willingness to bless this ministry with your beautiful talent."

Floyd smiled, as well. "Until Sunday. Be blessed."

"You, too, Floyd," Leilani said, her smile still in place.

"I told you," Allison sang. "Not only is Floyd handsome, but he's such a gentleman. He's the entire package, Lani."

"Allie, I will give it to you. He *is* fine. I'm not blind, nor am I dead." Leilani laughed. "He also appeared to be very intelligent and is oh so talented. He sang both selections. You didn't tell me the man could sing." Leilani giggled like a schoolgirl speaking about a crush.

"Sang?" Allison shouted. "WHAT?"

Leilani laughed. "Yes. Didn't you know he could sing?"

"Girl, no. Shut the front door! So you're telling me that fineeeeeee Floyd Hamilton is single AND he can sing?" Allison asked.

"He's talented, girl," Leilani answered. "He's going to be an asset to this ministry."

"Soooo, how was the chemistry between you two?" Allison inquired.

"What? Girl, I don't know," Leilani began. "I wasn't paying any attention to chemistry. We had a great conversation, though—just like I would with any other candidate being interviewed for a job."

"C'mon, Lani, it's me, Allie. Your best friend. Your sister. Save that formal mess for those church folks, girl. You know what I'm talking about," Allison teased.

"I mean, if you're asking if I thought he was attractive, yes, I did. He is a good-looking man indeed. But, honestly, I wasn't entertaining any of that," Leilani clarified.

"I respect that, Lani. Well, at least you noticed he was a handsome man. That's a start." Allison giggled.

"Allie, I'm not dead. I do know an attractive man when I see one. I'm just not ready to start dating anyone right now, if ever," Leilani retorted.

"Okay, girl. We'll see," Allison snapped back.

# Explore

It was going on almost two years since James' death, and Leilani hadn't been on a single date. She had not had a desire to seek the companionship of the opposite sex. She was often asked out on dates by some intelligent, handsome men who she would come across at the supermarket, gas station, bookstore, and even by single male members of her congregation. She never entertained the idea of dating anyone, though. That is until Floyd Hamilton became the keyboardist for the church.

Seeing him every Sunday took Leilani to another place—a mysterious place where she began daydreaming of exploring. But how could she think of another man? Was she disrespecting the memory of her late husband?

Her thoughts and sudden desires to have a male acquaintance in her life confused Leilani. It wasn't just any male acquaintance she thought of being with, though; it was Floyd Hamilton.

She had discussed her feelings with her grief counselor, and during one of their sessions, the counselor recommended she accept some of the offers for dates.

"Accept one or two a week, Leilani," she recalled her counselor saying. "It'll get you out of the house and away from your thoughts and work for a bit."

But, Leilani still was not up for the challenge of trying to date again. Although only shy of being thirty years old, she didn't like the idea of having to start over with someone new. However, she had a hard time keeping Floyd off her mind.

"God, give me a sign," Leilani replied aloud as she pulled her hair back into a ponytail. "I don't want to rush into anything. I don't want to lust after a man. I want everything to be right in your eyes," she continued to pray.

Leilani knelt on her knees. *My heavenly Father, Lord of Lord, King of Kings, you know my heart. You know my desires and your will for my life.*

*"You know that I am trying to live the life in which you've prepared for me. I do not want to entertain anything that is not of you. If my desire to be married again and to one day become a mother is not what you have in my future, remove those thoughts from me, Lord. Continue guiding my path where you want me to be. Guide me to whom you want me to be with, and he to me. Heavenly Father, all things will be done in your time and your time alone. Allow me the patience to wait on you and to accept what you have for me and me alone. In your glorious and majestic name, I pray. Amen."*

As Leilani stood to her feet, the telephone rang. Answering it, she responded, "Hello."

"Leilani?" asked a familiar male voice on the other end.

*Good Lord, you work fast,* Leilani thought. "Yes, this is Leilani," she spoke into the phone.

"Hi. This is Floyd."

"Good morning, Floyd. Is everything okay?" Leilani asked.

"Yes. I was just wondering what you were doing today," he began. "I have an extra ticket to a gospel concert at my mother's church and wanted to know if you'd like to accompany me."

"Oh, Floyd, how nice of you to offer, but—" Leilani began.

"You're busy?" Floyd interrupted.

"Uh, no…" Leilani continued, a little caught off guard by his abruptness.

"Then why not?" he asked matter-of-factly.

"Floyd, I don't know how to say this, but I don't think it would be a good idea for us to go out together," Leilani replied.

"I'm not asking you on a date, Leilani," he replied frankly.

Taken aback by his response, Leilani squeezed the phone's receiver, trying not to let it hit the floor. She felt like such a fool, jumping to conclusions like that.

"You're not?"

"No, I'm not. I just wanted to know if you were up to hearing some good southern gospel. I thought it would be something of interest to you—something we could maybe host at our church one day," Floyd continued. "But, since you—"

"Floyd," Leilani interjected, "when and where is the concert?"

There was a minute's pause before Floyd spoke.

"The concert is tonight, and it's in my hometown, which is about forty-five minutes from you. If this is too last minute, I do understand. I just found out an hour ago that my mother had extra tickets."

"Well, I could use a break and enjoy some good downhome singing. Can you give me directions to the location?" Leilani asked.

"If you aren't opposed to the idea, I would like to pick you up so we can ride together," Floyd responded.

Leilani's stomach tightened. *Is this a date? I know he said it wasn't a date, but he wants to pick me up from my house. Isn't that what happens on dates?*

Interrupting her thoughts, Floyd continued, "I could be there in an hour."

Leilani finally spoke up. "Okay. I'll be ready in an hour."

"You are in the townhomes out in Davidson, correct?" Floyd asked.

"Yes, 2211," Leilani replied.

"I'll see you in an hour," Floyd replied, hanging up the phone.

"It's a date!" Allison exclaimed.

"It's not a date, Allie. We're just going to hear good music, that's all," Leilani explained.

"Call it what you like, but I call it a date." Allison giggled.

"Allie, I haven't been alone with a guy other than James in years. I'm going to be riding in a car for forty-five minutes with this man. What do I say? What do I do?" Leilani panicked.

Although it was not a date, per se, Leilani could not help but feel a little apprehensive about the ride to and from the event.

"Just be yourself. Talk about things that you know about," Allison began. "If it's not a date, why are you so nervous?"

Leilani laughed nervously. "Don't start, Allie."

"I'm just asking." Allison tittered. "Sounds like you have first-date uneasiness."

"Would you stop taunting me?" Leilani joked.

"In all seriousness, Lani, just have fun. This is your first time one on one with a male since James' death. Just enjoy Floyd's company. He is such a gentleman. I know you're going to enjoy his company and the concert. Just let everything flow naturally and enjoy yourself. You need and deserve a good time," Allison replied.

"Thank you, Allie. I needed to hear that."

"You look lovely, Leilani," Floyd responded as Leilani closed and locked her front door.

She was wearing a flowing, knee-length lavender dress with a white shawl wrapped around her shoulders.

"You don't look too bad yourself," Leilani said while smiling at Floyd, who was wearing a pair of nicely pressed gray denim slacks and a light lavender shirt with the top button undone.

"Guess we had the same colors in mind," he commented with a smile as he opened the passenger side door.

"Looks like it," Leilani responded, getting into his white Range Rover Sport SUV.

Floyd got in and started the engine. "It's a nice scenic ride to my hometown. You shouldn't get too bored."

"I'm sure I'll be fine," Leilani replied, looking around his clean SUV with its leather aroma.

Leilani and Floyd rode in silence for about ten minutes before Floyd broke the silence.

"Tell me a little about you."

Leilani remained silent for a few moments, trying to decide how much she wanted to share.

Sensing her discomfort with his request, Floyd quickly added, "If I was out of line, I apologize."

"No," Leilani answered back. "It's just I don't know what you want to know."

"You can start with why you aren't married," Floyd candidly replied as if it was a question he had wanted to ask for a while.

"Wow! You just go for it, don't you?" Leilani joked.

"Mother always taught, if you want to know something, you must ask." He chuckled.

"Well, I'm a widow," Leilani began.

"Oh my! I'm sorry," Floyd replied, feeling guilty about asking the question.

"No. It's okay. I'm fine," Leilani continued. "I was married for a short while to a wonderful man, but soon after we returned from our honeymoon, we found out he had prostate cancer. By the time it was found, it had already spread to his bones and organs. It rapidly drained the life out of him."

"Oh, wow," Floyd replied, now feeling extremely regretful for opening old wounds. "Leilani, you don't have to continue."

"No. Honestly, Floyd, I'm okay. I have had enough time to heal, and my grief counselor said it's good to speak on it. God is so good because I can now speak about James without crying. There was once a time I couldn't even hear his name without bursting into tears. My wounds are healing. I am not fully healed. I still have scars, but I am slowly healing. Now when I talk about James and how wonderful he was, it makes me smile. I am so glad I had an opportunity to feel love the way he gave love to me."

"That's beautiful," Floyd replied. "Sounds like you two had a beautiful love affair."

"We truly did. He was such a support to me. He was a positive influence in my life, and I'm so glad I got to share part of my life with him." Leilani smiled. "Now I'm going to throw the same question back at you. Why aren't you married?"

Floyd chuckled. "I haven't found the right one."

"Just like that?" Leilani asked, expecting more.

"It's just that simple. God said a woman should be a helpmate, and I haven't found my helpmate. I've dated, but they all end up the same way with the woman pressuring me to marry her after only two or three months, not understanding my walk with Christ. I need an equally yoked woman, and until the Lord hand-delivers her to me, I'm going to continue living my Christian life and walk with Christ," Floyd explained.

"Amen," Leilani replied. "I agree with that. So where did you go to college?"

"I am a Morehouse man." Floyd smiled with pride.

"Is that so?" Leilani asked.

"It is so," Floyd replied, looking over at her. "What? You got something against Morehouse men?"

"No. It's not that at all. Why would I? After all, I'm a Spelman woman," Leilani responded.

"Get out of here!" Floyd exclaimed, and they both began to laugh.

"So, we got that Spel-House thing going on here, huh?" he asked.

"It appears that way," Leilani answered, smiling.

For the remainder of the ride, the two rode in silence.

"Mother, this is Prophetess Leilani Jordan," Floyd said, introducing Leilani to his mother, who was an attractive seventy-something, short, round, light brown woman with glasses.

"My, my, she's a pretty little thing," the elderly woman responded, extending her arms to hug Leilani.

"Uh. Thank you, ma'am." Leilani grinned and hugged the woman back.

Floyd grabbed his mother's hand and led her to her seat inside the sanctuary of his family's home church. He and Leilani took a seat beside her.

The pastor of the church stood in front of the audience and began to introduce the choirs that would be performing. Every performer that performed was better than the previous one. As Leilani rocked along to the songs, she could feel eyes on her. When she turned to her left, she caught Floyd starring at her. He smiled and quickly turned his attention back towards the stage where the performers were singing.

Leilani felt fluttering in her stomach. *Oh my gosh,* she thought. *This can't be butterflies.*

"Those were some incredible groups," exclaimed Floyd's mother, rocking in her rocking chair.

"They *were* good, Mother," Floyd responded as he settled on the front step of his mother's porch.

"Did you enjoy, young lady?" the elderly woman asked, looking over at Leilani, who was sitting beside her in the other rocking chair.

"Yes, ma'am. I had not heard singing that good since I was a child. It took me back to a time when I would hear my grandmother and her sisters sing at my grandfather's church in Georgia." Leilani smiled at the memory.

"Your grandmother was a singer?" Floyd asked.

"Yes. I don't know how familiar you are with old gospel groups, but my grandmother was the lead vocalist for the Connor Sisters," Leilani shared.

"I remember the Connor Sisters. It was three of them, wasn't it?" the elderly woman asked.

"Yes, ma'am. My grandmother, Louise Connor, and her sisters, Doris and Billie Mae Connor," Leilani replied.

"Oh, how I used to love to hear those ladies sing," exclaimed Floyd's mother. "That was during my time," she added, smiling.

"I feel out of the loop here," Floyd joked. "I have never heard of The Connor Sisters. Maybe you can let me hear their songs one day."

Leilani caught his eyes and quickly turned away. "Yes, maybe," she replied softly.

"Well, mother, it's been a nice visit, and dinner was delicious. No one makes meatloaf and homemade mashed potatoes like you do, and you still make the best pound cake in the state of North Carolina." Floyd smiled as he bent over to kiss his mother on the cheek.

"Hush up, boy, with all that silly talk. But you are right. I still got." The elderly woman chuckled. "That's why you're my favorite son," she added, then smiled and hugged his neck.

"Mother, I'm your only son." Floyd laughed aloud.

"It was a pleasure meeting you, baby," Floyd's mother said, smiling at Leilani.

"The pleasure was all mine, Mrs. Hamilton." Leilani smiled back at her, then reached down to hug the woman. "Thank you for being so hospitable."

"Make sure you come back to see me," the elderly woman continued. "Next time, I'm going to make you some peach cobbler."

Leilani grinned. "That sounds like a date. Peach cobbler is my favorite."

As soon as Leilani and Floyd reached the bottom step of the front porch, Mrs. Hamilton called Floyd back up to her and whispered something in his ear. When Floyd returned down the steps, he had a smirk on his face.

Looking back up at his mother, he told her, "You're always right. We'll see if you are this time. I love you, Mother."

"Thank you for the invitation, Floyd. I didn't realize how much I needed that break from my everyday life. A much-needed break." Leilani smiled. "Thank you."

As Floyd stood in front of her, Leilani could not believe the urges she was feeling in her body. What was this man doing to her?

"No problem. I enjoyed myself as much as you. Hopefully, it will not be our last outing together," Floyd responded while looking down at Leilani, who stood a mere five-foot, two-inches.

Leilani didn't know what to say. She was speechless. Was he asking her out?

"Leilani," Floyd said, interrupting her thought, "are you okay?"

"Uh...yes. I'm sorry. I think I'm a little tired," Leilani spoke up. "I need to shower and get some rest."

Perplexed, Floyd replied, "Okay."

He did not want to pressure Leilani into going out with him again. He started thinking that maybe she hadn't enjoyed their time together as much as he had.

"Well, I don't want to hold you. Have a good evening."

Floyd turned and began walking back towards his SUV parked in her driveway.

"Floyd," Leilani called after him.

Floyd slowly turned around, and the two stared at each other for a minute before Leilani said, "I really, really enjoyed myself."

"So did I," Floyd answered back with a smile and a thumbs-up.

"Allie, I blew it," Leilani whined.

"Lani, you did not. You told him you had a good time," Allison reminded her, trying to calm her friend.

"But he was trying to ask me out again, and I just ignored him," Leilani continued. "See, this is the reason I didn't want to go."

"Lani, you enjoyed yourself, and Floyd enjoyed himself.

That's all that matters," Allison replied. "Floyd knows what you've been through, and I know he knows you're uneasy about dating and getting involved."

"Allie, how do you know all of this?" Leilani asked.

"He told me," Allison replied honestly.

"He what?" Leilani asked, gripping the phone tighter.

"Yup. On his ride home, he called me. He likes being in your presence, Lani," Allison began. "Please don't let him know I'm sharing this information with you. But Floyd said from the moment he interviewed with you that he knew there was something special about you."

Leilani was flabbergasted. She could not believe what her friend was saying to her.

Allison carried on. "He said that spending time with you today and having you meet his mother confirmed the way he had been feeling about you from the moment he laid eyes on you. Girl, those are his words, not mine."

"So his mother must have said something to him about me when she called him back on the porch," Leilani told her.

"I think she did," Allison responded. "He didn't tell me what, but he said his mother is never wrong. He listens to a lot she has to say."

"Oh my, Allie. How am I going to face him knowing all of this now?" Leilani asked.

"You're going to act as if I didn't tell you a word." Allison laughed. "Seriously, just act normal."

"You're right," Leilani replied. "However, I must admit I am flattered by what you just told me, and if I can let you in on my little secret, I think I like Floyd, too."

Allison laughed on the other end of the phone.

"So is that my 'thank you' that I said you'd be saying to me when you were preparing to interview Floyd?"

Leilani started laughing, too.

"I guess it is, Allie. Thank you for introducing me to Floyd."

"I will pray for you, Lani. I'll pray that your spirit is ready and that the Lord will allow you both to let down your guards and enjoy what I know the Lord has for you both, which is another chance at love," Allison expressed sincerely.

"I will accept that prayer, Allie," Leilani replied, hanging up the phone.

# The Kiss

"I don't know any other women, Leilani, that I would feel comfortable taking," Floyd declared.

Hesitantly, Leilani replied, "Floyd, I don't mind helping you out, but I can't go to your company's Christmas party with you."

"Why?" Floyd asked. "You would be doing me a huge favor. I don't have a girlfriend, and I don't have a wife. You are the only woman I've been spending my time with these past few months. We will be going together as 'friends' if you need to put a title on something."

"Look, Floyd, you don't take your 'friend' to your company's Christmas party. There will be wives, girlfriends, fiancées, and me...the 'friend'," Leilani answered back. "What's wrong with going by yourself?"

Floyd sat back on the sofa, put his hands behind his head, and looked over at the pretty woman sitting next to him.

"I don't want to go alone. I want you to go with me," he replied like a five-year-old child begging a parent to do something they were told they couldn't do. "We've been spending a lot of quality time together, Leilani."

Leilani stared at the handsome, bright-eyed man in front of her. She knew where this conversation was headed, but was she ready? Should she ask him to leave her home or let him continue expressing his thoughts?

Interrupting her thoughts, Floyd continued, "I knew from the moment I met you that I wanted to get to know you better. A man knows a good woman when he sees one, and you are a good woman. You are a woman of God. You are loyal; you are caring; you are giving; you are dedicated; and you are everything I have been searching for. Leilani, in you, I see a virtuous woman."

Leilani could not believe her ears. Just seven months earlier she was introduced to her new keyboard player, and now here he was, like a knight in shining armor, sitting before her expressing his feelings for her. She was speechless.

*Was she ready for this? How do you respond to someone who you have been longing to be with for so long but fighting your desires?*

As she often did, she shut off her emotions and responded, "We don't need to get into all of this, Floyd. FINE! If it's that serious, I will go with you to your company's Christmas party."

"Get into what, Leilani?" Floyd asked. "I think it is that serious, and we need to discuss what's going on here."

He turned and grabbed both of her small, manicured hands.

"Floyd, what *is* going on here?" Leilani asked uncertainly.

"We see each other at church. We work on church events together. We have gone to dinner several times, and I've been to your mother's home on a few occasions. Isn't that what friends do?" she asked, trying to downplay the times they've spent together.

"Leilani, why?" Floyd asked.

"Why what, Floyd?"

"Why are you pushing me away? I see the way you look at me. I'm not blind. I know the feelings I have for you, and I know you have some type of feelings for me, too. Why can't you give us a chance? We have something special here."

"Because I can't," Leilani replied, pulling her hands away from him and walking over to her living room window that overlooked the lake in her community.

Floyd got up and walked over to stand behind her. Leilani could smell the scent of his cologne, which sent chills up and down her spine.

*Oh my gosh, is that Ralph Lauren Polo Blue he's wearing?*

"I know you've gone through a lot with the loss of James. I can't imagine losing the love of my life the way you lost James. But, I also can't imagine having the woman of my dreams finally enter my life, and I don't fight to keep her in my life," Floyd began. "I didn't know James, and I can't speak for him. But, as a man of God—and you say he was a man of God, as well—I do not think he would want you to grieve over him forever and let life pass you by. I'm quite sure he wants you to be happy, and I can make you happy."

Leilani turned to face Floyd. She could not believe what she was hearing.

"I'm not James, Leilani, and I never will be. But, he and I have something in common, and that's that we both adore everything about you." Floyd continued softly, "All I ask is for you to allow me to be the man that the Lord has for you at this point in your life. Allow me to make you smile every single day of your life. Allow me to comfort and take care of you. Allow me to make all your fears disappear."

He placed both of his hands on her shoulders.

"I want to be that man for you, Leilani. No, correction. I *am* that man for you. The Lord crossed our paths for a reason. Give me a chance to be the man for you and only you. Let me be your second time around. That's all I'm asking for—a chance to give you the love and support you deserve."

Tears began to well up in Leilani's eyes. Everything Floyd had just professed to her was everything she wanted for her life—everything she had wanted with James. And here she was years later, faced with everything she ever dreamed of in a man. But, the man wasn't James.

She closed her eyes and tears rolled down her cheeks.

"I can't believe this is happening to me again," she said, softly crying.

"Leilani, please trust me. I am not going anywhere. I'll never say goodbye and lose you. I want to love and take care of you," Floyd replied, wiping away her tears. "I beg you. Please don't push me away. What we have here is forever, and my heart won't let me let you get away."

Leilani looked up at the handsome man standing before her, and no words were needed. They stared at each another until Floyd tenderly placed Leilani's face in the palm of his hands and softly kissed her on the lips.

Leilani felt her stomach tighten. Floyd grabbed her and held her close, nestling his head in her neck and losing himself in her fragrant sweetness. When he lifted his head, his brown eyes wandered over her in a way that made Leilani's stomach quiver.

*Those darn butterflies*, she thought. She shivered as he held her close.

He suddenly lowered his long eyelashes and in a hoarse voice said, "So does that mean I have a date for my party?"

Clearing her throat, Leilani replied, "I guess it does."

# 'Til Death Do Us Part

"Lani, can you believe you're doing this again?" Allison asked while zipping up her best friend's beautiful champagne-colored lace dress.

Taking in a deep breath, Leilani smiled. "I can't. I feel like I'm in a dream. You're lucky if you get one true love in your lifetime. Some people never get one, and here I am getting a second chance at love, marrying one of the best men I have ever met."

"Floyd is a good guy. The Lord has truly blessed you, girl. Twice." Allison smiled. "Now, it's time for him to send one of his sons my way."

"I am so very blessed. That's why I have not questioned any of this. I have come to the realization—and at the pleas of Floyd—to just let go and let God. And that's what I am doing. I don't know how I got on this ride, but I'm going to enjoy it until it's no more." Leilani admired herself in the mirror.

"You look absolutely beautiful," Leilani's mother expressed as she entered the room in the church where Allison was assisting Leilani with getting dressed.

"Thanks, Mommy," Leilani replied, hugging her.

"If only your father could be here to see his baby girl." Leilani's mother smiled. "He would be just as happy as I am."

Bishop Bassett, who was twenty years Leilani's mother's senior, had been suffering from Alzheimer's disease for several years. He was now at the point where he was bedridden and had lost all his memory. Still, Leilani's mother religiously visited him every day to read the Bible to him and sing some of his favorite hymns. Although almost 94 years old, he still was a very handsome, distinguished man with a pleasant demeanor and that charming smile he had always displayed.

"Mommy, please don't make me cry," Leilani told her.

"I won't, my dear," the older lady replied, dabbing her eyes with a lace cotton handkerchief.

"I guess we're next," said a male voice from the doorway.

The notable-looking older man who had a gray beard stuck his head in the room where the ladies were waiting and smiled.

"I guess so, Uncle Leon," Leilani responded, smiling back at him as she grabbed hold of her mother's younger brother's hand.

The double doors of the church opened, and with the people in the sanctuary standing in the pews on both sides, all Leilani could see was her handsome groom at the front of the church dressed in a well-tailored black suit.

As Leilani approached the altar, she could see Floyd mouth the word, "Wow!"

Once she and her uncle made it to the front of the church, the pastor began to speak.

"Who giveth this woman to this man?"

Leilani's mother stood and replied, "I, her mother, and her father, Bishop Bassett, giveth her to this man."

Leilani turned to face her mother and smiled.

Her uncle kissed her cheek and placed her hands into Floyd's. After patting Floyd on the shoulder, he took his seat next to his sister.

The pastor continued. "Before I go any further, it is my understanding that you both have vows that you would like to share. At the request of the groom, the bride will go first."

Leilani smiled. "Me first?"

Floyd smiled and nodded.

Holding Floyd's hand tightly, she began. "Floyd Bernard Hamilton, my love, you are my constant friend, my faithful partner, and my loyal love. In the presence of God, our family, and friends, I offer you my solemn vow to be your faithful partner in sickness and in health." Leilani paused, tears welling up in her eyes.

Floyd smiled and squeezed her hand to reassure her that she was doing good.

Leilani continued. "I promise to love you unconditionally, support you in your goals, and honor and respect you. I promise to laugh with you and cry with you.

You came into my life when it was dark with no hope of light ever coming in. Your torch of light that was in the distance eventually came to the forefront, and I am so happy you pushed until you were in front of me, lighting up my entire life."

By this time, Leilani could not stop the tears from falling down her face.

"Floyd, entreat me not to leave you or to return from following after you. For where you go, I will go, and where you stay, I will stay. Your people will be my people. We will praise our God together as one. And where you die, I will die, and there I will be buried. May nothing but death part me from you."

As she finished her vows, there was not a dry eye in the church, including Floyd, who had a tear rolling down his cheek.

The pastor, who was also a little choked up, slowly moved forward. Clearing his throat, he said, "Floyd, your vows."

As the pastor stepped back, one of Floyd's groomsmen pulled a chair to the front of the church. Floyd walked Leilani over to the chair and sat her down in front of the piano.

"For my vows, I wrote a song for my bride. All that I feel will be expressed through the words I sing," Floyd announced, sitting down at the piano.

He began playing a soft, slow tune, and then that beautiful voice of his started to croon.

*"Without saying a word, you light up my world. It's hard to explain what I hear when you say nothing at all. The smile you*

put on my face, the truth in your eyes, lets me know you'll never leave me."

Leilani loved to hear Floyd sing. He had such calm joviality to his voice. It reminded her of Babyface whenever he opened his mouth, and he melted her heart every time he sang.

*"The touch of your hand says you'll catch me when I fall. And we need not speak at all, as I know what's being said between your heart and mine. You are mine, and I am yours; and from this day forth, there is only you and me. I love you more than you'll ever know, so take me. I'm yours, forever and ever. All my love, I give to you."*

After Floyd finished stroking the piano keys, he stood up, grabbed hold of Leilani's hand, and walked with her back to the altar.

The pastor smiled as he continued officiating the ceremony.

"Leilani and Floyd, no other human ties are more tender. No other vows are more sacred than these you are about to assume. You are entering into that holy estate, which is the deepest mystery of experience and the very sacrament of divine love."

Floyd smiled down at Leilani.

"Floyd, will you take your bride's left hand?"

Floyd released Leilani's right hand and held her left hand tightly.

"Floyd Bernard Hamilton, what symbol do you bring as a pledge of that sincerity of your vows?" asked the pastor.

"A ring," Floyd replied, placing a five-carat, platinum diamond ring with a beautiful pearl on Leilani's finger.

"Leilani Michele Jordan, what symbol do you bring as a pledge of that sincerity of your vows?" the pastor repeated.

"A ring," Leilani responded, smiling as she placed the platinum wedding band with diamonds on Floyd's finger.

"Rings have historically been the sign of authority used to seal documents and proclamations," the pastor continued. "Do you now accept this authority in your life?"

Together, Floyd and Leilani replied, "We do."

"With that being said, Floyd and Leilani have consented to holy matrimony and have thereto confirmed the same by giving and receiving each one a ring. By the authority committed unto me, I now pronounce you husband and wife, in the name of the Father, the Son, and the Holy Spirit. Amen. You may now kiss your ever so beautiful bride," the pastor concluded.

"Oh boy," Floyd uttered, then laughed before bending over to place a soft, lingering kiss on Leilani's lips.

The guests cheered as the two stood before them kissing. Leilani slowly pulled away and managed to wipe a little lipstick off Floyd's lips before he grabbed her hand and lifted both of their hands together for all to see their unity.

Leilani glanced over at her Allison, who was her maid of honor, winked at her, and mouthed, "Thank you."

She and Floyd then walked out of the rear of the church, hand in hand.

# Honeymoon Night ~ Love is in The Air

"I can't believe we're married." Leilani sat on Floyd's lap, securely anchored by his firm grip, in their honeymoon suite at The Ritz-Carlton.

"Believe it," Floyd breathed into her ear while kissing her neck.

He had waited so long for this moment and did not want to do a lot of talking.

A warm pleasure swathed Leilani's entire body as her husband's kisses lengthened, and she melted from the honeyed feeling of passion. Her arms wrapped around his neck, and her fingers gripped his ear. After a while, she felt him slip the spaghetti strap of her nightgown off her shoulder. His fingers began to stroke her shoulders, her arms, and eventually landed on her bare breast. His thumb brushed against her nipple, and at that moment, a sensational feeling began to rise inside of her.

"This is heaven." She gasped, filled with joy.

Floyd groaned and buried his face in her hair. He held her against him so firmly she could barely breathe.

"My goodness!" he exclaimed. "You smell divine."

"My heart is pounding nonstop," Leilani whispered, arching her body closer to him.

"Mine, too," he said, groaning deeply. "Leilani, I want you. I need you."

"Then take me," she responded in a whisper.

Floyd laid her on the king-sized bed, switched off the lamp beside the bed, and stripped off his t-shirt.

The first time Floyd made love to his wife, he was driven by passion. He all but tore off her nightgown to get to her. He had been building a desperate quench inside for Leilani ever since the day he took her to his hometown for the church gospel concert.

After the initial fury, Floyd slowed his pace to enjoy the moment with his new bride. He wanted to savor her sweet glory and concentrate on pleasing her. His mouth searched; his hands explored; his body was hard and satisfying.

This went on for well over an hour until neither had the strength to move. Leilani snuggled against him in the dark room. She was wonderfully tired and could not think straight, but who was trying to think during that joyful moment? All she knew was that she was truly blessed to get a second chance at love. She was glad she did not allow her fear of loving again stop her from taking a leap of faith with the man who God had for her.

On his deathbed, James asked her to promise him that she would love again, and she had kept her promise. She loved Floyd Bernard Hamilton, and he loved her back.

When she woke the next morning, she felt lazy, a little smug, and fortunate to have a husband who knew what he was doing in the bedroom.

Leilani lay snuggled close to her husband, who appeared to be sleeping like a baby. His scent still lingered from the night before, evoking delicious memories of the love they made.

Floyd wasn't sleeping, though. His eyes were closed, but he was enjoying the moment with his wife. He was thinking about her positive, kind heart and how she made him smile. Her petite body curled up against him. Her captivating scent. How her fingers felt like magic on his skin. Her soft, smooth lips nuzzling him just where it felt the best.

Leilani enjoyed a quick daydream about what would happen the remainder of their honeymoon, and it sent chills up and down her spine.

This had to be a dream!

# Pitter-Patter

Leilani and Floyd spent a week in beautiful Miami, Florida, for their honeymoon. It felt like it came and went by quickly.

Back home in North Carolina, their things were scattered all over their new home, but Leilani never had the slightest inclination to complain. After all, they had just merged two homes. She sold her townhome, and Floyd made his house a rental property. Leilani treasured the intimacy of sharing living space with Floyd.

That morning, the sun was so bright that it woke Leilani, and she discovered Floyd had already left. Like always, he had been careful not to wake her when he got up and dressed for work.

While lying in bed, Leilani felt the churning of nausea that she had felt every morning for the past few weeks since returning from their honeymoon. She dove off the bed and dashed straight for the bathroom, where she was pugnaciously sick.

She pulled herself up off the floor and rinsed her mouth out with water, then gargled with mouthwash, and washed her drained face with a washcloth.

She stared at herself in the mirror before opening the drawer and pulling out a pregnancy test. *I guess I need to use this,* she thought, looking down at the box.

"Girl, will you eat those saltine crackers and drink that hot tea," Allison joked, pushing a plate of crackers in front of Leilani. "So when are you going to tell Floyd?"

Reaching for the saltine cracker, Leilani began to nibble on it. "I don't know."

"What do you mean, you don't know? The doctor just confirmed what the home pregnancy test said. You're pregnant, girl!"

"I know," Leilani whispered.

"It's his baby, too!"

"I know, Allie! I just don't know if he's ready to be a daddy yet."

"What? He doesn't want children?"

"No, that's not it. He just may not be anticipating any children this early in our marriage."

"Well, whether he's anticipating it or not doesn't mean he won't be glad about it. Sis, that man loves you."

"I know, and I love him."

Leilani could not believe it. She was having a baby. Leilani was frightened with the knowledge that a life was growing inside of her body. At the same time, she was thrilled she had a part of Floyd growing inside of her.

"Floyd, will you be right home after work tonight?" Leilani asked.

"Of course. I got to get home to you," Floyd replied. "Is everything okay?"

"Everything is fine," Leilani responded, pressing her hand to her abdomen to assure herself that she was still carrying Floyd's baby. She was beginning to show slightly but hadn't yet told Floyd.

Time was passing. She and Floyd had already been married going on four months.

"I just have something to discuss with you tonight."

*She sounds serious. What is it? I know she doesn't want to divorce me, so what could it be?* Floyd wondered.

"What is it?" he asked. "Give me a hint."

"I can't. I have to do this face-to-face."

"Leilani Hamilton, what do you have up your sleeve?" Floyd asked jokingly.

"Nothing," Leilani teased.

"You're up to something," Floyd replied.

"You'll have to wait to find out, now won't you?" Leilani giggled like a schoolgirl taunting a friend.

"Okay, pretty woman. For you, I'd wait a million years. I'll plan to be home a little early tonight. I love you," Floyd told her.

"I love you, too. See you later," Leilani replied before hanging up the phone.

After doing her hair, Leilani looked at herself in the floor-length mirror in their bedroom. Her face looked perfect. She wore a scoop-cut maxi cami dress that made her silhouette look relaxed, and the soft coral color complemented her dark brown skin and was femininely flattering.

She went into the bathroom to reapply her light pink lip gloss, then returned to the bedroom. Swallowing hard, she sat on the bed in their master suite, waiting on Floyd to enter the house.

A few minutes passed, and she heard his vehicle pull up.

Moments later, Leilani heard Floyd calling for her.

"Leilani, where are you?" Floyd called out, locking the front door of their house.

Leilani could hear Floyd at the front of the house, as she waited anxiously in the bedroom.

The house was dark except for the light coming from the stove in the kitchen. Right when Floyd flipped the light switch, he stubbed his shoe against what appeared to be a baby car seat.

*What in the world?* Floyd thought as he continued to walk through the house.

On the kitchen counter, he saw jars of baby food and baby bottles.

"Leilani!" he called out again. "Where are you?"

Leilani sniggered as she heard him getting closer to their bedroom.

Floyd continued further into the house. As he approached, he noticed baby clothes laid across the back of the sofa. Shaking his head slowly, he began to smile.

Floyd finally arrived at their bedroom and opened the door to find Leilani standing before him in a sexy sundress.

Leilani forced herself not to look away from his gaze. The way he looked at her always made her feel like she was naked. His stare was like one she had never experienced in her life, not even with James. It was as if he could see her entire soul.

"What are you up to, beautiful?" he asked, grabbing his wife and hugging her.

"Why do I have to be up to something?" Leilani asked with a mischievous grin.

After a moment, Floyd got serious. "You have something to tell me. What is it?"

Leilani began to feel panicky. "What I'm trying to tell you is…you're going to be a daddy."

He let out a yell, and his hand moved to cup her belly like a basketball.

"I knew something was going on here," he said while gently rubbing it.

"We weren't using birth control."

"I know," he said. "No complaints from me. I'm going to be a daddy!"

His amazed tone reassured her that all was well.

"A baby! I knew you were up to something when I almost tripped over a car seat. Then there's baby food and bottles all over the kitchen counter, not to mention the baby clothes on the sofa."

"So you don't mind?"

"Mind? My sweet angel, there's no other woman I ever want to be the mother of my children but you," Floyd continued, stroking her stomach with his fingers.

His hands extended down to her waist and tightened. As he pulled her against him, she unzipped his pants. He began kissing her behind her ear, and his heart started doing flips.

"Can I go there with you?"

As she was working his shirt off his muscled arms, she kissed his throat and chest.

"Yes," she replied between kisses. "We can go there. I can handle it."

As she continued placing kisses all over his body, she felt him shiver. Looping her arms around his neck, she pressed her body against his.

"I love me some you."

Floyd felt all his resistance melt in the sweet desire he had for his wife. He picked Leilani up, laid her gently on their bed, and wrapped his entire being around her. His hands lingered over her hips and legs before settling on her stomach.

My Lord, she loved herself some him, and she knew she would never love that way again. He was indeed the man for her.

Floyd sighed her name as he felt her arch her body against his, and their mouths met in a soft, wet kiss.

They lost themselves in one another, and their lovemaking took them to heights neither had ever felt.

"Are you okay?" Floyd asked as they laid together.

Leilani's hand was still caressing his muscular arm. She couldn't get enough of him.

"Are we still allowed to make love while you're pregnant? I wasn't thinking."

Leilani smiled lazily. "I'm still early in the pregnancy. We're good."

Floyd cupped his hand around her nape and looked at her intensely with a focused love that Leilani felt deep in her soul.

"Thank you."

A lump formed in her throat. "No, thank you, baby."

His heart melted. He had never seen the type of love in any woman's eyes towards him like the love he saw in his wife's eyes that night.

She tilted her head up towards him. "I can't believe we are going to have a baby."

"I know. We're going to be parents."

His mouth covered hers, and hours later, they were both still busy expressing thanks to each other.

# What God Has for You

"You did good, baby." Floyd smiled while rubbing Leilani's head.

Leilani smiled back at her husband and said, "Zora Nicole."

"Yes, Zora Nicole. You have made me the happiest man in the world," Floyd told her.

"She's a fine baby girl," Leilani's mother expressed. "You did well, Leilani."

"Thanks, Mom."

"Did Mom get off safely?" Leilani asked.

Her mother had flown in from Atlanta for the birth of her first grandchild.

"She did," Floyd replied, walking over to Leilani's bedside. "You know she'll be back in a few weeks after she finishes handling your dad's affairs."

Leilani's father had passed away a month before Zora Nicole was born. He passed in his sleep at the assisted living facility.

"I can't believe it," Leilani replied. "We have a baby."

"I can believe it. What God has for our lives will be, and Zora Nicole is what the Lord had planned for us," Floyd replied, rubbing his baby daughter's cheek with his finger.

She was a beautiful baby—a mixture of both he and Leilani, with a head full of jet-black hair like her mother.

Cradling her daughter in her arms, Leilani looked down at the tiny bundle of joy that God blessed them with.

Several years prior, she thought her life was ending. Now, here she was with a new life. A new beginning. What a blessed woman she was. She had it all. A successful career. A beautiful church family. A loving and adoring handsome husband. A loving mother and a best friend who never left her side. And now, she had a beautiful, healthy baby girl all her own.

*Thank you, God,* she thought. *Thank you for allowing me to trust again and for giving me the strength to take another leap of faith on love.*

# God's Promise to You

Dear Readers:

Thank you for reading my first book, *A Leap of Faith*. I hope you enjoyed Leilani, Floyd, and the other characters as much as I enjoyed creating them.

I also hope for those of you wanting to find your one true love, that this book gives you hope and keeps you encouraged as you wait on being found. Remember that when God created this world, HE knew it was not good for man to be alone. HE instituted marriage in the Garden of Eden.

At times, you may be gripped by anxiety when you think of your future. I'm no different and share that same emotion at times. Rest assured, though, that the Lord knows you need a partner in your life. HE knows the longings of your heart, and HE most definitely knows what's best for you.

Keep the faith, my dear readers. GOD, as you will see in scripture, has blessed many of HIS people with the

RIGHT life partner and made them happy, and HE can do the same for you through HIS angels.

Every good gift comes from the LORD, and HE never denies HIS children joy and happiness. Commit your future into HIS loving hands!

Always Be A Blessing,
Tam Yvonne

P.S. – I would love to hear your thoughts about the book. Please write to me at TheAuthorTamYvonne@yahoo.com.

# About The Author

Tam Yvonne, enjoys reading and cannot resist a good romance novel, has been writing ever since she could put a sentence together. She spends countless hours people watching—looking for story ideas and characters to develop. Her upbringing of being an Army brat and traveling the world has helped with her research for her books.